GALILEO'S
Leaning Tower Experiment

A Science Adventure

Wendy Macdonald
Illustrated by Paolo Rui

iːi Charlesbridge

For Maxie—W. M.

To my beloved wife, Vicky, and our child, Leo,
who fill my heart with wonder—P. R.

Published by Charlesbridge
85 Main Street
Watertown, MA 02472
(617) 926-0329
www.charlesbridge.com

Library of Congress Cataloging-in-Publication Data
Macdonald, Wendy (Wendy Margaret)
  Galileo's leaning tower experiment : a science adventure / Wendy Macdonald;
illustrated by Paolo Rui.
     p. cm.
   ISBN 978-1-57091-869-8 (reinforced for library use)
   ISBN 978-1-57091-870-4 (softcover)
1. Mathematical physics–Juvenile literature. 2. Gravity–Juvenile literature.
3. Galilei, Galileo, 1564–1642–Juvenile literature. I. Rui, Paolo, ill. II. Title.
QC20.M28 2009
531'.5–dc22   2008010652

Printed in Singapore
(hc) 10 9 8 7 6 5 4 3 2 1
(sc) 10 9 8 7 6 5 4 3 2 1

Illustrations done in acrylics on canvas
Display type and text type set in P22 Mayflower and Concorde BE
Color separations by Chroma Graphics, Singapore
Printed and bound by Imago
Production supervision by Brian G. Walker
Designed by Sarah McAbee and Martha MacLeod Sikkema

Massimo threw a stone off the bridge and watched it fall—
plop—into the river.

"Hey, Massimo! Why don't you come with me?" called a boy
herding a flock of goats across the bridge.

Massimo waved. "Thanks, but I have to wait for my uncle's boat."

Massimo threw another stone. *Plop*.

"That looks like a good game," a stranger said.

"It's not a game, sir," Massimo replied. "I'm watching how fast the stone falls."

4

"Why does that concern you?" the man asked.

"Because I'm waiting for my uncle," Massimo explained.

"Every market day I have to drop this food for him to eat."

He looked up the river. "Here comes his boat now."

Massimo picked up a wheel of
cheese and a loaf of bread. Just before the
boat passed under the bridge, he dropped them.
They landed on the boat with a single thud.

"Strange how the two things landed at
the same time," the stranger said.

"Of course they did," replied Massimo.
"I wouldn't let my uncle's food fall into the river."

"But the cheese is heavier. It should have fallen
faster and landed first," the man said. He stroked
his beard. "Could Aristotle be wrong?"

"Good morning, Professor Galileo!" a group of noisy students called out, laughing and pushing each other as they crossed the bridge.

Massimo stepped away from the man. "You're a professor?" he asked.

"I am," the man said. "But this morning it seems I am your pupil." As Galileo walked slowly away, the rowdy boys followed.

Massimo walked to the marketplace to meet his sister, Angela. As they packed up the donkey cart, Massimo said, "I just met a professor from the university. He was very interested in how I dropped the bread and cheese onto Uncle's boat."

"And why should he be interested in that?" Angela asked. "Those professors, they waste their time thinking."

"Perhaps they do," admitted Massimo. "He didn't even know how to drop food from a bridge!"

All week Massimo was busy with his chores on the farm. At the end of the week, he went to the bridge again. He smiled shyly when the professor walked up to him.

"Are you dropping more food for your uncle?" Galileo asked.

"Yes, sir," Massimo answered. "Here he comes." The boat moved swiftly down the river. Massimo waited for just the right moment. Then he dropped the bread and cheese.

Galileo listened carefully as the packages again landed with one thud. He shook his head and asked, "How could Aristotle be so wrong?"

"Is this Aristotle a friend of yours?" asked Massimo as they walked to the marketplace.

The professor laughed. "Hah! I wish I had such a friend," he said. "Aristotle lived almost two thousand years ago. Many people believe he was the smartest man who ever lived. He explained how and why things happen."

"Like how things fall?" Massimo asked.

"Exactly," Galileo replied. "He said that heavy things fall faster than light ones do. For the second time, you have shown me that they do not.

"I will tell you what I think," Galileo said, stopping at a fruit seller's cart. He picked up a pear and let it fall to the ground.

"That pear fell because it had to," Galileo said. "The earth has a force that pulls all things toward it, unless"—he threw a grape in the air and caught it in his mouth—"unless something stops it as it falls."

"Why did Aristotle say that things fall at different speeds?" asked Massimo.

"I don't know," Galileo said, "but we know that the bread and cheese fell the same distance to the boat, and we heard them land at the same time, so the speed of the fall must have been the same, too."

Galileo said good-bye, and Massimo walked
over to where his sister was packing up to go home.

"Who was that?" asked Angela.

"That was Professor Galileo, the man I told
you about," Massimo said.

"He looks too young to be a professor,"
she said, frowning. "Don't believe everything
he tells you. Everyone knows that people
only gain wisdom with age."

That afternoon Massimo told his donkey all about it. "People say Aristotle was very smart, but I wonder if he ever tested his ideas. Then he would have seen what really happens." The donkey shook his head and snorted.

"Hmm," said Massimo. "I've only tried dropping bread and cheese. Maybe other things fall differently."

He found a hammer and a broken buckle. He held them up and let them go at the same time. "I think they landed together, but I couldn't really tell," he said. "Maybe I need to be higher up."

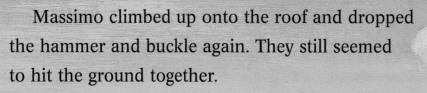

Massimo climbed up onto the roof and dropped
the hammer and buckle again. They still seemed
to hit the ground together.

Angela came out to feed the chickens. "What are you
doing?" she asked. Massimo told her about Aristotle and
the speed of falling objects.

Angela shook her head. "If you ask me, this Aristotle
was right. You know how slowly a feather falls."

"Let's try it," Massimo said. He picked up a chicken
feather and dropped it with the hammer. The hammer fell
straight to the ground, but the feather drifted lazily down.

"You're right," Massimo said, bowing his head.
"Things do fall at different speeds. Aristotle was
as wise as everyone says. Oh, I must tell Galileo."

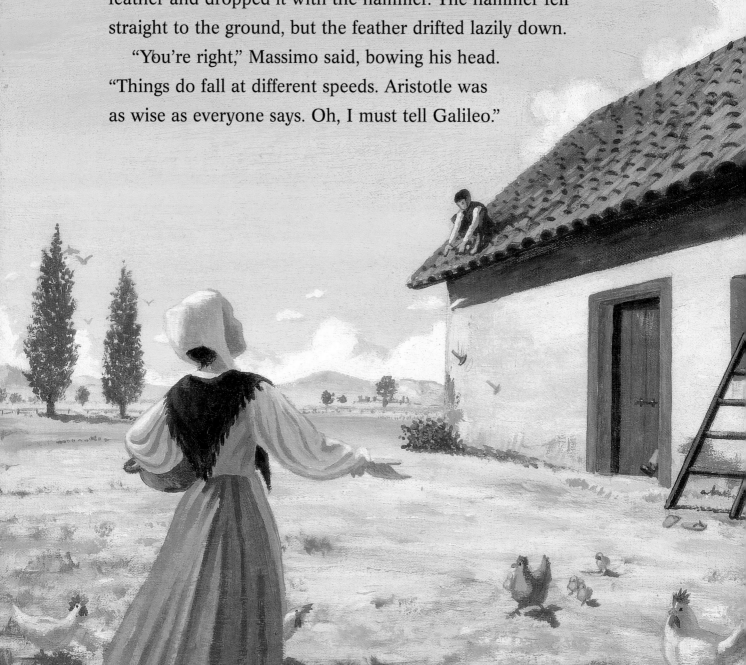

The next day Massimo looked for Galileo on the bridge and at the market. The professor did not appear. "I must look for him at the university," Massimo decided.

Shabby farm boys were not allowed at the university. But Massimo took a deep breath and walked into one of the huge marble buildings. Crowds of people stood everywhere, talking and laughing. No one noticed him.

Massimo hurried through the courtyard. He stopped only to admire a statue with letters carved into the stone below it.

"I wish I could read this," he said quietly as he ran his hand across the letters.

"What are you doing there?" a voice growled.

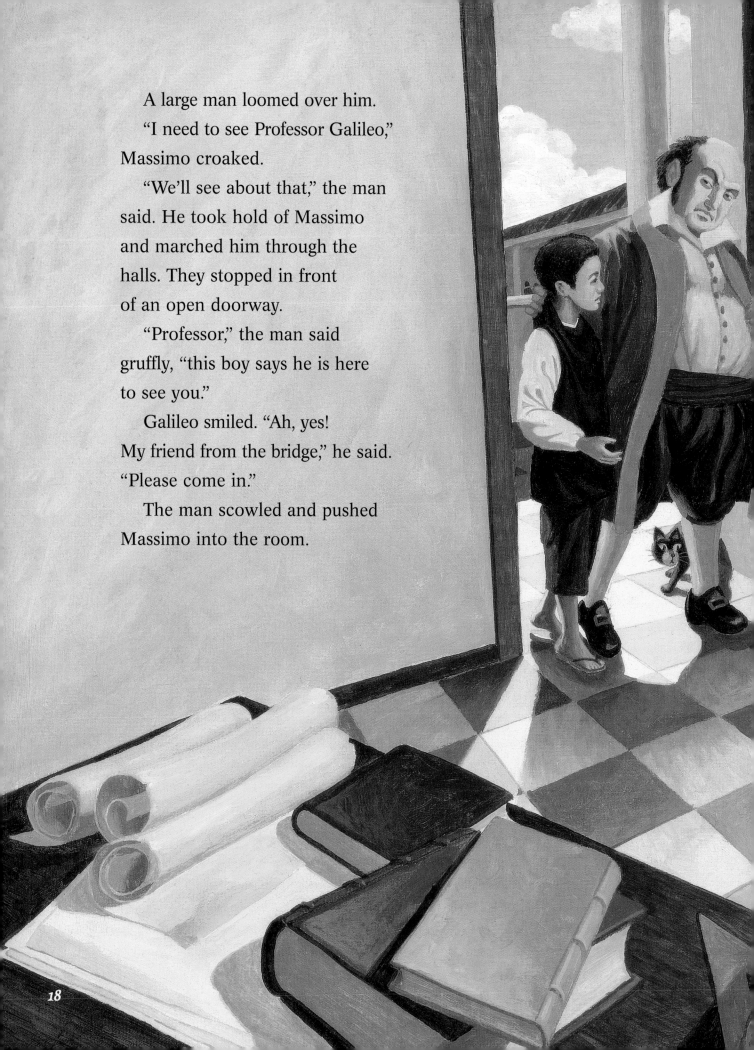

A large man loomed over him.

"I need to see Professor Galileo," Massimo croaked.

"We'll see about that," the man said. He took hold of Massimo and marched him through the halls. They stopped in front of an open doorway.

"Professor," the man said gruffly, "this boy says he is here to see you."

Galileo smiled. "Ah, yes! My friend from the bridge," he said. "Please come in."

The man scowled and pushed Massimo into the room.

Massimo stared at the books and papers that filled the office. A thick book on the desk looked as if it had more words than all the ones he knew.

"What brings you here?" Galileo asked kindly.

"I'm sorry to trouble you, Professor," Massimo began, "but it looks as if Aristotle was right after all." He told Galileo about the buckle and the feather.

Galileo chuckled. "Interesting. I have been dropping
things, too." He handed Massimo a sheet of paper
and a rock. "Drop these."

Massimo held them as high as he could
and opened his hands. The rock fell to the
floor, while the paper floated down slowly,
just like the feather.

Galileo crushed the paper into a ball.
"Try it again."

This time both objects hit the floor together.

"What happened?" gasped Massimo.

"It's the air," Galileo replied. "Air is all around us in what looks like empty space. A piece of paper has a large surface, so when you drop it, the air holds it up a little, and it takes longer to fall."

Massimo nodded slowly. "But by crushing the paper, you made the surface smaller, so the air didn't hold it up so much." He picked up the paper ball. "The paper and the rock fell at the same speed. So Aristotle really was wrong."

"Yes, but I must prove it," Galileo said. "It is not easy to change people's minds."

"You could show them by dropping things in front of them," Massimo said.

"Yes, but where?" Galileo wondered.

The bells in the old tower began to ring. "The bell tower!" Massimo exclaimed. "It's the tallest building around."

Galileo smiled. "I will invite everyone from the university. Will you help me?"

23

The next day Massimo hurried through his chores and went into town. Many people were already gathered around the tower. As Massimo walked through the crowd, he heard bits of angry conversation.

"Galileo is crazy."

"How dare he challenge the great Aristotle!"

"I am named after Aristotle. I will not let this professor make a mockery of my name."

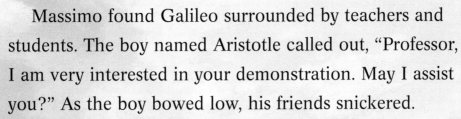

Massimo found Galileo surrounded by teachers and students. The boy named Aristotle called out, "Professor, I am very interested in your demonstration. May I assist you?" As the boy bowed low, his friends snickered.

Massimo made his way through the older boys. "I am here to help the professor," he announced.

Galileo smiled at Aristotle. "Thank you, but I have an assistant."

Galileo and Massimo rolled several cannonballs into the tower. The student named Aristotle stuck his head in the doorway and sneered at Massimo. "One of those balls weighs as much as you do. I will help."

"No, thank you," Massimo said and pushed the older boy out. Quickly he swung the door shut and bolted it.

One by one, Massimo carried the heavy cannonballs to the top of the tower.

At the top Massimo looked down at the sea of tiny, upturned faces. "Professor, it looks as if all of Pisa has come to see your demonstration!"

He and Galileo set up two long boards. Between the boards they placed a cannonball and a smaller musket ball. Galileo waved to the crowd and told Massimo to stand ready.

"Now!" Galileo shouted. They pulled away
the board in front and pushed the back
piece forward. The two balls rolled
over the edge at the same moment.
Time seemed to slow down as
Massimo watched the balls
fall. Then they hit
the ground with
a single thud.

At first there was complete silence. Then people began to argue about what they had seen. They started to chant, "Again, again!"

Galileo and Massimo repeated the demonstration over and over. Finally even the student named Aristotle agreed: the large ball and the small ball landed together. They must have fallen at the same speed!

When Galileo and Massimo came down
from the tower, the crowd cheered.

Galileo and Massimo shook hands.

"Well done, my young friend," Galileo said.
"You have helped uncover a great secret just by asking
questions and paying attention to how things really
happen. You have the kind of mind I enjoy teaching.

Would you like to be my student?"

"Oh, yes!" Massimo answered. "There's so much I want to find out! How fast do things fall? Do they speed up on the way down? What happens if I throw something instead of just dropping it?"

Galileo smiled. "At the university you can explore all those things and more. Truly, you will help us observe common things in uncommon ways."

This story takes place in 1589, an exciting time of many new scientific discoveries. At the age of twenty-six, Galileo had just become a professor at the University of Pisa. He began doing experiments to explore how and why things move. Legend has it that Galileo dropped weights from the Leaning Tower of Pisa to test his ideas. Historians are not sure whether this event actually occurred because no eyewitness accounts exist.

In this version of the story, Galileo and Massimo (a fictional character) compare the speed of two falling objects to see if one lands before the other. If you try their experiment, you will find that the higher you hold the objects, the easier it is to see if they land at the same time. Try it with different pairs of objects. If they land together, they are traveling at the same speed.

Galileo also experimented with rolling balls down a ramp. He measured the speed and found that the closer the ball got to the bottom of the ramp, the faster it went. We call this change in speed *acceleration.*

Galileo went on to make many other important discoveries through observation and experimentation. Today Galileo is considered one of the founders of modern science.

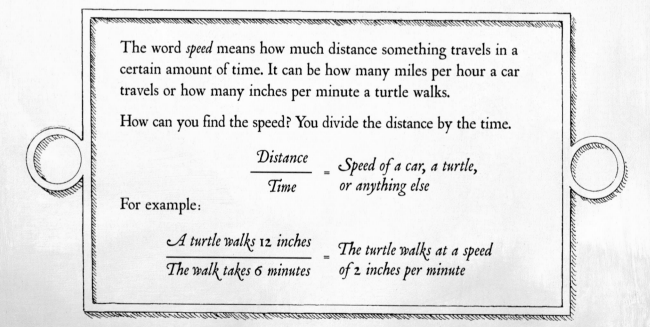

The word *speed* means how much distance something travels in a certain amount of time. It can be how many miles per hour a car travels or how many inches per minute a turtle walks.

How can you find the speed? You divide the distance by the time.

$$\frac{Distance}{Time} = \text{Speed of a car, a turtle, or anything else}$$

For example:

$$\frac{A\ turtle\ walks\ 12\ inches}{The\ walk\ takes\ 6\ minutes} = \text{The turtle walks at a speed of 2 inches per minute}$$

A note about education in the 1500s: For a bright farm boy to go to school was possible, but very unusual. Only the wealthy (and only boys) typically went to the university.